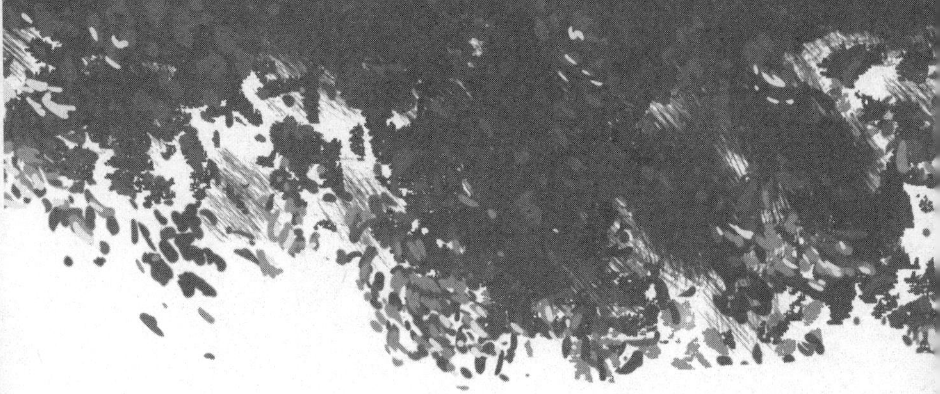

Willow Moss & the Vanished Kingdom

Also by Dominique Valente

Starfell #1: Willow Moss & the Lost Day

Starfell #2: Willow Moss & the Forgotten Tale